For my daughters, Allison and Sarah.—C.B.
To my family, the best ones. To all the Monsters, the naughty ones.—O.V.

STERLING CHILDREN'S BOOKS
New York

An Imprint of Sterling Publishing
1166 Avenue of the Americas
New York, NY 10036

ISBN 978-1-4549-1103-6

Distributed in Canada by Sterling Publishing
c/o Canadian Manda Group, 664 Annette Street
Toronto, Ontario, Canada M6S 2C8
Distributed in the United Kingdom by GMC Distribution Services
Castle Place, 166 High Street, Lewes, East Sussex, England BN7 1XU
Distributed in Australia by Capricorn Link (Australia) Pty. Ltd.
P.O. Box 704, Windsor, NSW 2756, Australia

For information about custom editions, special sales, and premium and corporate purchases,
please contact Sterling Special Sales at 800-805-5489 or specialsales@sterlingpublishing.com.

Manufactured in China

Lot #:
10 9 8 7 6 5 4 3 2 1
05/15

www.sterlingpublishing.com/kids

MIND YOUR MONSTERS

by Catherine Bailey • illustrated by Oriol Vidal

STERLING CHILDREN'S BOOKS

New York

Wally enjoyed a quiet, normal life . . .

. . . until one day monsters invaded his small town
and made a mess of everything.

Zombies knocked over lampposts.

Werewolves chased the mail carrier.

Vampires scared kids at the park.

Wally tried to ignore them.
But the monsters were hard to ignore.

They were loud and clumsy and smelled like rotten eggs.

Wally tried talking to them.

But the monsters wouldn't listen.

Wally tried to fight fire with fire.

That didn't work at all.

Wally tried everything a kid could think of . . .

. . . . from tricks to treats.

Nothing worked.

Finally the townspeople had had enough.
The grown-ups took a vote and agreed to leave town.
But a giant ogre blocked the only road out.

The blob squished all the airplanes.
And a mutant octopus sank all the boats.

Wally was fed up.

"Will you PLEASE stop breaking all our stuff?" Wally shouted.

"Okay," blurbled the octopus.

Everyone froze.

"Please move," Wally said to the ogre.
The ogre moved.

"Please pick up the lampposts," Wally said to the zombies.
The zombies picked up the lampposts.
"Thank you," said Wally.

The townspeople crowded around Wally.
"How did you do it?" they shouted. "What's your secret?"

Wally grinned and said, "Magic."
The grown-ups stared at Wally.

"The magic word: PLEASE!" Wally explained.

"Of course! The magic word!" cheered the townspeople.
Then everyone started using it.

Soon all the monsters were on their best behavior.

In fact, the monsters and townspeople started having a lot of fun together.

But eventually it was time for the monsters to leave.
They were homesick for their caves, planets, lairs, and holes.

Monsters are monsters, after all.

All the monsters and all the townspeople gathered to say
good-bye to one another. Everyone shook hands
(and tentacles and claws) and wiped away tears.

Wally cleared this throat.
"Thanks, everyone, for playing nice and
getting along. I'm glad we've become friends."

Then Wally smiled and asked,
"Will you come back and visit us?"

The Monsters stayed silent.
Cyclops blinked.
The zombie scratched his head.

Ahem.